PUFFIN BOOKS
THE TWIG THING

Jan Mark grew up in Kent and attended the Canter-
bury College of Art. She went on to teach art at
Gravesend. She started her writing career in 1973,
and since then has written a large number of highly
successful books, for which she has been awarded the
Carnegie Medal and other prestigious prizes. She
spent two years as writer-in-residence at Oxford Poly-
technic and now lives in Oxford.

Jan Mark

The Twig Thing

Illustrated by Sally Holmes

PUFFIN BOOKS

PUFFIN BOOKS

Published by the Penguin Group
Penguin Books Ltd, 27 Wrights Lane, London W8 5TZ, England
Penguin Books USA Inc., 375 Hudson Street, New York, New York 10014, USA
Penguin Books Australia Ltd, Ringwood, Victoria, Australia
Penguin Books Canada Ltd, 10 Alcorn Avenue, Toronto, Ontario, Canada M4V 3B2
Penguin Books (NZ) Ltd, 182–190 Wairau Road, Auckland 10, New Zealand

Penguin Books Ltd, Registered Offices: Harmondsworth, Middlesex, England

First published by Viking Kestrel 1988
Published in Penguin Books 1990
10

Printed in England by Clays Ltd, St Ives plc

For Rosie and Ella

Contents

Upstairs and Upstairs

As soon as Rosie and
Ella saw the house they
knew that something was
missing. The house was tall
and thin. It stood on the
pavement.

Rosie said, "Where is the garden?"

"Gardens are at the back," Ella said.

"It's got a lot of windows," Daddy said.

They stood in the street and counted: one door and seven windows.

There was no garden at the front of the house, only a paved place for the dustbin and three steps up to the door. The top step was where a milk bottle lived. It looked as if it had lived there for a long time.

"Let's go in," said Daddy. "It's our house now."

Inside was a hall, a kitchen and a dining-room.

Rosie said, "Where's the garden?"

"Gardens are at the back," Ella said.

So they looked out of the
window in the dining-room,
but there was no garden
at the back, only a long
drop to the ground.

"There is a garage
underneath," Daddy said.
"Come upstairs."

Upstairs was a big
living-room and two small
rooms.

"This room is Ella's,"
said Daddy, and he opened
the door of the first small
room.

"This one is Rosie's," he said, and he opened the door of the next room. It was even smaller.

Ella said, "Where's the garden?"

Rosie said, "Gardens are at the back," because Ella had said that gardens are at the back. So they looked out of the living-room window, but there was only a very long drop to the ground, and no garden.

"Come upstairs," Daddy said.

Rosie said, "More upstairs?"

Ella said, "In our last house you could only go upstairs once."

"There must be a garden
somewhere," Rosie said.

"There is a garden," said
Daddy.

They went upstairs
again. There was one big
bedroom and one very big
bedroom and a bathroom.

"This room is for visitors," Daddy said, and he opened the door of the big bedroom at the front. Then he opened the door of the very big bedroom at the back. "And this one is for me," he said.

Ella said, "It's too big for only you."

"For me and my books," said Daddy.

Rosie said, "Where's the garden?" They looked out of the window of Daddy's bedroom because it was at the back. There was no garden, only a terribly long drop to the ground.

Rosie said, "This is a very dangerous house."

22

"Come upstairs," said Daddy.

Ella said, "More upstairs? These stairs only go into the ceiling."

Daddy said, "No, they don't. Look again," and he pointed.

At the top of the stairs was a door. It was lying on its back in the middle of the ceiling. Daddy went up the

stairs and opened the door.
Rosie and Ella climbed
behind him. They looked
up and saw the sky.

"Here you are," Daddy
said. "This is the garden."
They looked round and
saw the garden.
It was on the roof.

Sky High

Rosie said, "This isn't a garden, it's a pavement."

Ella said, "It is a garden. There are plant pots."

"There are no plants," said Rosie.

29

"Stay away from the railings," Daddy said, so they went to the railings. Ella went to the front railing and Rosie went to the one at the back. On both sides there was a fearfully long drop to the ground.

Rosie said, "This is the most dangerous house I have ever lived in."

Ella said, "I wish I could fly."

Daddy said, "Don't try.
You must never come up
here without me."

"I don't ever want to
come up here," Rosie said.
"I want to go back to the
other house and play on

the grass. There isn't any
grass here. It's cold and
windy and it's not a real
garden."

"It will be," Daddy said. "We will make it into a real garden in the spring. It won't be cold and windy then."

Ella said, "It won't be

spring for ages. Can we
have tea?"

So they went downstairs,
and downstairs again, and
down some more stairs,
until they found the
kitchen.

But all the mugs and
plates were in boxes and
they could not find the
teapot. Daddy made tea in
the milk jug and they
drank it out of eggcups.

There was only one
chair. Daddy sat on the
chair. Ella sat on his right
knee and Rosie sat on his
left knee and they all ate
sandwiches.

"Tomorrow the furniture will come," Daddy said.

Ella said, "But where shall we sleep tonight?"

"You two can sleep in my bed," Daddy said. "It's already here."

Rosie said, "Where will you sleep?"

"I shall hang upside-down from the ceiling," Daddy said. "Like a bat."

Ella helped Daddy to
wash up. Rosie went to the
front door because there
was something she wanted
to look at. In the front door
was another, very small,
front door.

Rosie said, "What is this
for?"

"That is a catflap,"
Daddy said.

Ella said, "We haven't
got a cat."

"Then we must get one,"
said Daddy. "We can't
have a catflap without a
cat."

Rosie opened the catflap and looked out into the dark street. It was still windy and cold. The wind blew across the top of the milk bottle and made it moan.

Rosie felt sorry for the milk bottle, all alone in the dark on the cold step. She fetched some crumbs from the kitchen and threw them out of the catflap, on to the top step, in case the poor milk bottle felt hungry in the night.

The wind blew litter
along the pavement.

A paper bag went past,
and a black feather, and
then a cardboard box. The
wind blew a twig thing

along the street and it stuck
behind the dustbin.

"Come to bed now," said
Daddy, so Ella and Rosie
went upstairs, and upstairs
again, to the bathroom.

Then they went
downstairs, once, and got
into Daddy's bed, which
was in the living-room for
now.

Daddy gave them a hug
and sang to them until they
went to sleep.

The Twig Thing

Next morning Rosie
woke up early and went
downstairs. In the dining-
room Daddy was asleep.

He was not hanging from
the ceiling, he was on the
floor in a sleeping bag.

Rosie went past very
quietly and opened the
catflap. Outside on the step

the milk bottle was still
there, but the crumbs had
gone.

And the twig thing was
still there, stuck behind the
dustbin. Rosie could see it

49

properly now. It had a
neck, and two front legs,
and two back legs, and a
long stiff tail, but it wasn't
an animal, it was a twig. It
looked cold.

Then Ella got up and
jumped on Daddy, so
Daddy got up too and they
had breakfast.

After that a van arrived
with all the furniture in it,
and two men carried the

furniture inside. Daddy helped them. While the front door was open Rosie slipped out to the dustbin and fetched the twig thing.

"Don't run off and get lost," said Daddy, when he saw her. So Rosie went and sat in the kitchen with Ella and watched the furniture go by.

When all the furniture was in, the men went away with the van.

"Lunch time," Daddy said. He had been unpacking, so for lunch they had eggs in the eggcups and made tea in the teapot and drank it out of mugs.

"What have you got there?" Daddy said.

"This is my twig thing,"
Rosie said. "I found it by
the dustbin. It came last
night."

Daddy looked at it.
"Let's put it in water," he
said.

But they could not find a
vase.

"I know," said Ella, and went to the catflap. She put out her arm and brought in the milk bottle. Rosie filled it with water and put the twig thing in the water.

Daddy put the milk bottle on the window sill and the twig thing stood there on its tail, with its four legs stuck out and its neck in the air.

"It looks like an animal," Ella said. "A very thin animal with only bones and no fur."

"I shall call it Twiggy," Rosie said.

"Let's call it Puss," said Ella, "until we get a cat."

"I should call it May," said Daddy, "because I think that's what it will be."

So the twig thing stood on the window sill in the

kitchen. Rosie was glad
because it was warm now,
and the milk bottle was
warm too.

Every time she went into
the kitchen she said,

"Hello, May."

"I wish it could talk,"
Rosie said. "I wish it would
say, 'Hello, Rosie'."

"It's too busy growing to
talk," Daddy said.

"I'm growing," said
Rosie, "and I can talk."

"But you aren't a twig
thing," said Daddy. "You
are my beautiful Rosie."

"What about me?" said
Ella.

"You are my lovely Ella
and you are growing too,"
Daddy said.

"The twig thing grows
faster than us," said Rosie.

"If you didn't talk so
much," said Daddy, "you
might grow faster too."

The Tree

After a while Ella went
to her new school. Rosie
went to playgroup in the
morning and in the

afternoon she went to a
lady down the road who
looked after children.
Daddy went to work.

In the evening they all came home and had tea together.

They got a cat. It was a thin little cat and they

called it Twiggy. Twiggy
went in and out of the
catflap, out in the morning,
back again at night.
Daddy said that she was
going to work too.

On the kitchen window sill the twig thing stood in the milk bottle. It was getting bigger. At the end of its legs grew little green buds, like paws. At the end of its neck was a much bigger bud, like a head.

Twiggy was growing bigger too. Sometimes she brought home a mouse. That was Twiggy's work, catching mice.

Outside in the street the wind stopped blowing and the sun shone. It shone into the kitchen window and the buds on the twig thing opened. They were leaves. More leaves grew along its legs, like green fur.

One day Rosie went into the kitchen and said, "Hello, May."

"Look at its head," said Daddy, and he pointed. The twig thing's head was covered in small white flowers.

"I said it would be May,"
Daddy told her.

The sun went on shining.

"Can we go into the
garden yet?" Ella said.

"I think we can now,"
Daddy said, so they all
went upstairs, upstairs and

upstairs, to the roof.
Twiggy came too.

They counted the plant
pots.

"Six," said Rosie.

"Seven," said Ella, who
went to school. "We must
buy some seeds."

"We must buy some earth," Daddy said, and next day he brought home a bagful. Rosie had never seen earth in a bag, before. It was called Potting Compost.

Rosie said, "Where are the seeds?"

"We will all go out tomorrow and choose them," Daddy said.

"I want to plant something now," said Rosie.

"Then we shall," Daddy

said. "Come on up to the roof."

So they all went up to the roof with Twiggy. Daddy opened the bag and put some earth into the biggest plant pot.

"Now fetch your twig thing," said Daddy to Rosie, and she went downstairs, downstairs and downstairs to the kitchen.

The twig thing stood in its milk bottle on the kitchen window sill. The

flowers had died but the
leaves were green and
strong. Rosie lifted it down
and carried it up to the
roof.

Daddy said, "Now, put it

in the plant pot," and Rosie
did it. The twig thing stood
in its new pot and looked
like a little green tree.

"It may grow into a real
tree," said Daddy, "if we
hope very hard and treat it
kindly."

So they all stood round
the twig thing in its pot,
and held hands and hoped
very hard.

It was the first plant in
the garden.